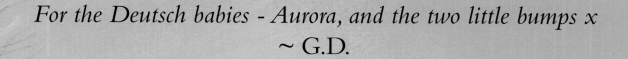

*For the Deutsch babies - Aurora, and the two little bumps x*
~ G.D.

*For my lovely friend, Dianne*
~ A.E.

**tiger tales**
5 River Road, Suite 128, Wilton, CT 06897
Published in the United States 2018
Originally published in Great Britain 2018
by Little Tiger Press
Text by Georgiana Deutsch
Text copyright © 2018 Little Tiger Press
Illustrations copyright © 2018 Alison Edgson
ISBN-13: 978-1-68010-101-0
ISBN-10: 1-68010-101-3
Printed in China
LTP/1800/2208/0218

For more insight and activities,
visit us at www.tigertalesbooks.com

# The Snow Rabbit

by Georgiana Deutsch

Illustrated by Alison Edgson

tiger tales

Bear was ALWAYS GRUMPY.
He had a big, furry frown and a sulky scowl.
And whenever he felt REALLY, REALLY
grumpy, he would give a grizzly, grumbly . . .

RRRRROWL!
Shhhhh!
Bear's in a REALLY bad mood!
ONLY BEARS ALLOWED

The animals didn't dare to go near Bear's beautiful yard. Except for one very smiley Rabbit . . . .

Good morning, Bear!

GO AWAY!

"Poor Bear," said Rabbit as she skipped away. "He needs cheering up!" And Rabbit knew just what to do!

Don't do it, Rabbit!

I have a great idea!

That night, Bear couldn't sleep.
He grouched and grumbled and
looked out his window. And there,
in the moonlight, was . . .

The trees trembled and shook at the sound of Bear's rumbling roar, until . . . CRASH!

A pile of snow landed right on top of Bear *and* the snow rabbit!

Oh, no! Now I have soggy fur AND a squished snow rabbit!

The next morning, Bear woke up in a **VERY BAD MOOD.** He peeked outside, frowning as he saw the leaning snow rabbit sitting sadly in the sunshine.

"FOX!" Bear growled. "Did YOU
build a snow rabbit in MY yard?"
Fox gulped. "N-n-n-no!" he stuttered.
Bear harrumphed and stomped off.
"It must have been Badger," he grumbled.

Bear stormed up Badger's path.

…RABBIT!

"Hello, Bear!" smiled Rabbit, hopping up. "Did you call?"
"YES!" bellowed Bear. "YOU put a snow rabbit in my yard!"

"I-I-I thought it might make you smile!" said Rabbit hopefully.
Bear took a deep breath.
The animals covered their ears.
"Well, it did **NOT** make me smile," Bear growled . . . .

"IT MADE A GIANT MESS! And you're going to help me fix it! OR ELSE!" Bear turned and marched home. Rabbit blinked in amazement.

"We can fix this!" Rabbit offered when
she saw the squished snow rabbit.
And together, that's what they did.

Then, when the snow rabbit looked just right,
they made a snow bear. And for the first time
in a long time, Bear forgot to be grumpy.

That night, Bear couldn't sleep. He stood at his window and gazed out at the snow bear and the snow rabbit, standing together in the moonlight. A slow smile spread across Bear's face. "It feels good to have a friend," he said.

And that gave Bear a WONDERFUL IDEA.

Chuckling to himself, Bear pulled on his boots . . .

marched into his yard . . .

I'd better change THIS!

and got to work on
his mysterious plan.

The next morning, the animals
were in for a surprise . . . .

And with so many new friends,
Bear was NEVER grumpy again!